For Cory

Text copyright © 1994 by Cynthia Rogers Erkel. Illustrations copyright © 1994 by Michael Erkel. All rights reserved.
This book, or parts thereof, may not be reproduced in any form without permission in writing from the publisher.
G. P. Putnam's Sons, a division of The Putnam & Grosset Group, 200 Madison Avenue, New York, NY 10016.
Published simultaneously in Canada. Printed in Hong Kong by South China Printing Co. (1988) Ltd.
Book design by Gunta Alexander. The text is set in Horley Old Style.
Library of Congress Cataloging-in-Publication Data
Erkel, Cynthia Rogers. The farmhouse mouse / by Cynthia Rogers Erkel; illustrated by Michael Erkel.
p.   cm.   Summary: A tiny fieldmouse causes a big commotion when he tries to spend the night in a quiet farmhouse.
[1. Mice—Fiction.   2. Humorous stories.   3. Stories in rhyme.]   I. Erkel, Michael E., ill.   II. Title.
PZ8.3.E789Far 1994 [E]—dc20   92-27040   CIP AC ISBN 0-399-22444-0 10 9 8 7 6 5 4 3 2 1 First Impression

THE FARMHOUSE MOUSE

Cynthia Rogers Erkel

illustrated by
Michael Erkel

G. P. Putnam's Sons · New York

On a bitter cold and blustery evening,
when even the trembling tree limbs were freezing,
a walnut-sized field mouse was headed for home

He tumbled and scrambled, half running, half blown.
And just as the night began filling with snow,

he spied a warm farmhouse, its gold eyes aglow.

So, he made himself flat and squeezed under the door,
then he scampered upstairs to the highest floor.
But when poor Gertrude Howell heard a noise in the attic,

she jumped up in a wild panic.
"HERBERT!" she called. "Did you hear that?
There's no mistake, I heard a rat!"

So they went to the attic and laid three traps.
But the mouse stole the cheese for himself:

Snap! Snap! Snap!
Gertrude looked up. "*Three* rats!" she counted.
"Let's set up more traps on the double!" she shouted.

But the more they set up, the more the mouse snacked.
Darting and snatching, he set off the traps.
"*FIVE RATS!*" Gertrude screamed. "NOW WHERE IS THAT CAT?"

The field mouse had now found his way to the dishes.
There were pie crumbs and split peas and corn bread…delicious!

Soon the sound of his nibbling grew too loud to bear.
Gertrude snatched up a shoe, let it fly through the air.
The thud woke the cat from his comfortable dreams.
But a field mouse was not what he saw, it seems.

"EEEEooooowwwwwlll!" the cat cried, running into the hall,
where Herbert was giving the neighbors a call.

Jimmy brought Blackie and Norma, his hounds.
Then Mary brought Daisy, her pet skunk, around.

Now skunks make good ratters, anyone knows,

unless you're a dog with a sensitive nose.

Blackie and Norma made such a scene

that everyone thought, "Wow—those rats are *too mean*!"

The Howells just stood there and watched in the cold,
as the last of their friends disappeared down the road.

Then they turned toward the door, toward the army of rats
that had scattered their neighbors and withered their cat.

But just at that moment the field mouse ran by.
He stopped once and blinked his tiny black eyes.
Then he brushed off his whiskers and ran out the door;

a walnut-sized mouse, and that's all, nothing more.
"My, my," Gertrude chuckled, shaking her head.
Then she and Herbert went off to bed.

That night they slept tight in their quiet farmhouse.

And also, quite full, in his hole, slept the mouse.